The Alden Family Mysteries
by Gertrude Chandler Warner

THE BOXCAR CHILDREN
SURPRISE ISLAND
THE YELLOW HOUSE MYSTERY
MYSTERY RANCH
MIKE'S MYSTERY
BLUE BAY MYSTERY
THE WOODSHED MYSTERY
THE LIGHTHOUSE MYSTERY
MOUNTAIN TOP MYSTERY
SCHOOLHOUSE MYSTERY
CABOOSE MYSTERY
HOUSEBOAT MYSTERY
SNOWBOUND MYSTERY
TREE HOUSE MYSTERY
BICYCLE MYSTERY
MYSTERY IN THE SAND
MYSTERY BEHIND THE WALL
BUS STATION MYSTERY
BENNY UNCOVERS A MYSTERY

MYSTERY RANCH

MYSTERY RANCH

by Gertrude Chandler Warner

Illustrated by
Dirk Gringhuis

SCHOLASTIC INC.
New York Toronto London Auckland Sydney

ISBN 0-590-42687-7

Published by Scholastic Inc., 730 Broadway, New York, NY 10003, by arrangement with Albert Whitman & Company. THE BOXCAR CHILDREN is a registered trademark of Albert Whitman & Company.

31 30 29 5/9

Printed in the U.S.A. 40

First Scholastic printing, December 1989

Contents

CHAPTER 1

The Door Bangs

An exciting summer began for the four Alden children with the bang of a door.

The big house where they lived with their grandfather had been as quiet as a house can be with four children in it. Their cousin, Joe, had gone to Europe with his new wife, Alice. Everything seemed peaceful, until the afternoon when the door banged.

It was Mr. Alden.

Benny said, "Hi, Grandfather!"

"Hello," Mr. Alden answered.

That was all. He went straight to the front room and shut that door loudly too.

"Well!" thought Benny. "What in the world is the matter with Grandfather?"

He ran upstairs to the room where Jessie and Violet were reading.

"Listen!" Benny cried. "Something terrible must have happened to Grandfather. He banged the door, and all he said was 'Hello.' He always says, 'Well, hello, Benny, and how are you today?' "

Jessie shut her book quickly and sat up straight. "Did you tell Henry?" she asked.

"No," answered Benny. "I just told you, and that's all the time I had."

"Hen-ry!" called Jessie.

"What's the matter?" asked Henry, coming down the hall. He knew by Jessie's voice that something had happened.

"Benny says that Grandfather came in and banged the door, and hardly spoke to him."

Henry stood still in the door. "Where is our

grandfather now, old fellow?" he asked his little brother.

"In the front room with the door shut," Benny answered. "And a bang on that door, too."

"Oh dear!" said Henry.

"What can be the matter?" asked Violet. Her pretty little face was white.

"We should go talk to him," said Henry quietly.

The children looked at each other and started slowly down the stairs together. Henry took a deep breath and rapped on the door.

"Come in," Mr. Alden called. He sounded very tired. He was sitting with his head in his hands.

"Don't be afraid to talk to us, Grandfather!" cried Benny.

"That's right," said Henry. "We always tell you our troubles. Now you have a trouble, and we'll help you."

"I wish you could, my boy," said Mr. Alden sadly. "But I don't know what you can do."

The children sat down on the floor and waited quietly for him to go on.

"I got a letter about my sister. You didn't know I had a sister, did you?"

"No, Grandfather," said Jessie. "But we're a funny family. Once we didn't know we had a nice grandfather. And we didn't know that Joe was our cousin."

"That is true, my dear," said Mr. Alden.

"Where does she live?" Benny asked.

"Out west on a ranch. The nearest town is Centerville," Mr. Alden said. He looked very sad.

"Jane is old, and she is a very cross woman. The neighbor who stays with her is going to leave. Nobody will stay with Jane because she is so hard to get along with. She won't leave the ranch, and yet I can't let her stay there all alone."

"Why don't you go to see her, Grandfather?" Benny asked.

Mr. Alden gave a short laugh.

"Jane wouldn't let me in," he said. "She doesn't like me. I have not been very nice to her, either."

"Tell us about the ranch," said Jessie.

"Well, it's the old family ranch," said Grandfather. "I lived there when I was a little boy. When my parents and I came East, Jane stayed."

He stopped. He seemed to be thinking to himself, as if the children weren't there.

"For a while she did very well," he went on. "But later, she had to sell the cattle and the horses. She has only one old horse and some chickens now. She must be very poor, but she still won't take any money from me."

"Proud," said Benny.

"That's right, Benny. She's too proud to let me help her. Let me have time to think about this. You go eat your supper, and ask Mrs. McGregor to bring me a tray. I'll eat in here. You are kind children, but you can't help me now."

"But, Grandfather," began Benny.

"No," said Mr. Alden. "Go to supper like good children. I must think about this alone."

CHAPTER 2

The Letter

Nobody moved for a minute. At last Henry said, "Listen, Grandfather. We can't eat a thing if you stay here all alone. Do let us help you. At least tell us who wrote the letter."

Mr. Alden looked at each of his grandchildren. They were all watching him with loving eyes.

"Well," he said slowly, "have it your way. Maggie wrote the letter. She is the neighbor who stays with Jane. I have sent a nurse three times, but Jane always sends her back. She doesn't want anyone there, even to help her."

"Isn't it terrible to be like that?" asked Benny.

"Yes, Benny. It's a very sad thing," said Mr. Alden. "Jane was always hard to get along with."

"But what does Maggie say?" asked Henry.

Mr. Alden looked at his oldest grandson and pulled a letter out of his pocket. "Well, you may as well know the whole story," he said. "Here is her letter." He handed it to Henry.

Benny cried, "Read it out loud! Then we'll all know what it says!"

Henry looked at his grandfather. Mr. Alden nodded. Henry began to read.

"Dear Mr. Alden,

"I am writing to tell you that I cannot stay any longer with your sister. I do not get enough to eat. Jane is very cross to me, and she has many strange ideas. Now she wants to see some of your grandchildren. She is not sick, but she stays in bed all the time. I won't leave her until you send someone else, but you must do something."

For a minute nobody said a word. Violet was leaning on the arm of her grandfather's chair. She looked at him and said, "I think I know a way to help, Grandfather."

Jessie began to laugh. "Violet! Are you thinking what I'm thinking?"

"I guess so," said Violet, smiling at her older sister.

"I guess so, too," cried Jessie. "Grandfather, Violet and I would like to take care of Aunt Jane."

Mr. Alden was quiet.

"Please let us go, Grandfather," Violet begged.

"My dear girl," said Mr. Alden, "it isn't that I don't want you to go. I just wonder if Jane will be polite to you."

Violet said, "We're not worried about that. Jessie and I would be company for each other. And I like to take care of sick people."

"I know that well, my dear," said Mr. Alden. "Many times you have made me feel better when I was sick."

"Telephone, Grandfather!" shouted Benny. He

could never bear to wait. "Tell Maggie that the girls are coming, and everything will be all right forever and ever."

"Jane doesn't have a telephone," said Mr. Alden. He smiled at Benny's surprised face. Benny thought that everyone had a telephone.

"However, I could send a telegram," said Mr. Alden. "They send telegrams from the train station in Centerville."

"Let me look up trains," said Henry, getting up from the floor. "I wish I could go, too. I have never seen a ranch."

"I wish you could, too, Henry," said Jessie. "But it is better for just girls, isn't it, Grandfather? Four strange children would frighten Aunt Jane."

Henry had found a timetable. "There is a train leaving at six o'clock tomorrow that would take you there. You'd have to sleep on the train."

"We would love that," said Jessie.

"Well," said Grandfather slowly, "if you are really going, I should tell you some more. Maggie's

brother, Sam Weeks, lives next door with his wife. They are very kind people, and I am sure you can stay with them, if Jane isn't nice to you."

Mr. Alden already had another telegram in his mind, which he would send to Sam as soon as the children had gone to bed.

"There is just one thing you girls must promise me," said Mr. Alden. "Every day you must send me a telegram."

"Of course we promise," said Jessie.

"Come on, let's eat!" said Benny. "Can't you smell the ham and eggs, Grandfather? Don't you feel hungry now?"

"Why, yes, I think I do," said Mr. Alden, surprised. "I really think you two girls might do Jane more good than anyone else in the world."

Jessie looked at Violet with a smile, which said, "Won't we have fun?"

Violet was already thinking of her aunt as her dear Aunt Jane.

But then, Violet had never seen many cross people.

CHAPTER 3

A Cool Welcome

Such excitement! Mrs. McGregor, the housekeeper, packed a big lunch in a box. She handed it to Jessie with a motherly smile.

Benny peeked in the box and said, "If Aunt Jane doesn't give you enough to eat, that lunch will last you two or three days."

Mr. Alden took the girls to the train station. He watched them carefully as they took a seat together.

Jessie and Violet smiled and waved until they could not see their grandfather.

The hours passed quickly for the two girls, because everything was new and exciting. They noticed a young man who was reading a book. He was very tall. He had soft brown hair and brown eyes. Once he passed by them to get a drink of water and smiled at them.

The girls smiled back. When he took up his book again, Jessie whispered to Violet,

"He is very good looking, isn't he?"

They thought no more about the young man until they came to Centerville early the next morning. There the young man surprised them by saying, "I'm getting off here, too. May I take your bags?

"Why yes, thank you," said Jessie. "That blue one and the white one up there are ours."

"I could guess that," laughed the young man.

He lifted the bags down. He took both of them in one hand and his own heavy one in the other. The girls looked around the station platform for Maggie.

"Thank you for carrying the bags," said Violet. "It was very kind of you."

"Not at all," said the stranger, politely.

A voice behind them asked, "Are you Miss Alden?"

"Miss Alden?" said Jessie, turning around. "Oh, yes, I'm Jessie Alden. And this is Violet. Are you Maggie?"

"Yes, I'm Maggie. I'm very glad to see you."

The girls picked up their bags. This made them think of the young man. He had disappeared!

"Where did that man go?" Jessie asked. "The one who carried our bags?"

"I don't know," said Maggie. "Who was he?"

"I had never seen him before," said Jessie. "He was very polite, anyway."

"Not many people get off here," said Maggie. "I wonder why he came to Centerville."

"Well, as Benny would say, 'A Mystery Man,' " said Violet, smiling.

Maggie led the way around the station to a very thin black horse which stood in front of an old wagon.

"Get in," Maggie said. "There is only one seat, but we can all sit on it."

Maggie took the reins. The old horse raised his head and walked slowly down the road.

"He'll walk all the way home," said Maggie. "He's not like the horses we used to have. We had riding horses and a herd of cattle, and we raised wheat. It was a fine ranch in the old days. But now your aunt can't run the ranch any more. Did you know she is in bed?"

"Yes, Grandfather told us."

"Did he tell you that she doesn't want to eat, and she won't let me eat, either?"

"Yes. That seems terrible!" said Violet.

The horse stopped at the back door of an old brown house. The girls got out of the wagon. Maggie opened the back door and let them into the kitchen.

"Your Aunt Jane is in *there*," Maggie said. "Put your bags down. I'll go into her room and tell her."

"The girls are here," Maggie said to someone out of sight.

The two sisters went quietly into the bedroom. They saw a tiny woman half sitting up in a big, high bed. She was very thin, and she did not smile, even when she saw the two girls.

"So you're James Alden's grandchildren!" a sharp voice said.

Jessie went nearer the bed. "He is very worried about you, Aunt Jane," she said.

"Worried? Pooh!" said the little old lady. But she couldn't help liking that friendly voice saying "Aunt Jane." No one had talked so kindly to her in years.

She raised her head and asked, "What's the matter with the other girl? Can't she talk?"

"Yes," said Violet, smiling. "I shall talk so much you'll be tired of hearing me."

Miss Alden said nothing. But she found herself thinking, "I'll never be tired of hearing that soft voice."

"I'll put them in the big bedroom," Maggie said. "Is that all right?"

"Put them anywhere," said Aunt Jane. She turned her face to the wall.

Maggie went out and nodded at the girls to come, too.

"Ever see anyone as cross as that?" she asked.

"No," said Jessie. "We feel sorry for her."

Maggie led the way upstairs.

They went into a big room with many windows and a big high bed.

"What is really the matter with Aunt Jane?" asked Violet. "Is she very sick?"

Maggie looked at the little girl. "Well," she said,

"I don't think there's a thing the matter with her."

"But why does she stay in bed, then?"

"She isn't strong enough to get up now," Maggie answered. "There's nothing for her to live for. So she doesn't care about living. I suppose that's why she won't eat."

"Well, we are going to eat," said Jessie.

"I'm hungry now," said Violet.

"Let's go down to the kitchen, then," said Jessie.

As they went downstairs, Maggie said kindly, "You girls make yourselves right at home."

When they came to the kitchen, Maggie took one look out the window. She saw the horse still standing by the back door.

"Mercy! I forgot the horse!" she cried. And she rushed out of the door, leaving the girls alone.

It was then that Violet turned to look at her aunt's door. It was shut.

"Look, Jessie," she whispered. "Aunt Jane must have shut that door. It means that she can get out of bed if she really wants to."

CHAPTER 4

Aunt Jane's First Meal

Let's not wait for Maggie," Jessie said, in her businesslike way. "Let's get dinner."

Soon, Violet was busy beating eggs in a bowl. Jessie put butter in a big pan and set it on the stove. The girls put pieces of dry bread in the eggs and milk, and Jessie began to brown them in the pan.

"My, that smells good!" cried Maggie, coming into the kitchen. "*She* going to eat this?"

"No," said Jessie. "I'm just going to give her something to drink. But we'll eat first."

Violet had found a pretty blue cloth and some white flowers. She had set three places with fine old blue plates. A knife and fork were at each place, and a glass of milk.

"All ready!" Jessie said, with a smile. "Come on, Maggie, and sit down. I hope you'll have enough to eat tonight."

"It's the most I have had for two weeks, anyway," said Maggie. "You are a good cook for a young girl."

They did not hear a sound from the bedroom. At last, even Maggie couldn't eat any more.

"Now for Aunt Jane," said Violet, getting up. She opened the lunch box and took out an orange.

"I could drink that myself!" Violet said, watching Jessie mix the orange juice with a beaten egg.

Jessie knocked gently on the bedroom door.

"Well, come in!" said Aunt Jane. "Don't stand there knocking!"

Her voice was cross, but Jessie thought she had been lying there waiting for something to happen.

She put the glass on the table. Then she went over to the bed, and bent over the tiny little lady.

"Aunt Jane, this is delicious," she said. "Violet and I made it just for you."

Jessie went on, "Now I'm going to lift you up higher in the bed, so you can drink better."

To the old lady's surprise, Jessie lifted her in her strong arms as if she were a child. Then she took the glass and sat down by the bed.

"Drink it slowly," she said. "As Benny would say, 'Don't rush it.' "

"Who is this Benny?"

"Well," began Jessie. "Benny is—" she stopped. "It's so hard to tell you about our brother Benny."

Violet came in, folding up the blue tablecloth. She acted as if she had always lived there.

She said, "Benny is the funniest boy you ever saw, Aunt Jane, and he is good, too. He can always make people laugh. He loves our dog, Watch. Benny and Watch almost talk to each other. Benny always looks for Watch if things go wrong."

Jessie noticed that her aunt was drinking the egg and orange; and not very slowly, either. She seemed to be very hungry.

"Who else is in your family?" asked Aunt Jane.

"Well, there's Henry," said Jessie. "He's our oldest brother. He is very clever, and very kind and thoughtful. He can make Benny mind, too, without being cross."

"If your brothers are like you, I'd like to see them, too. Take the glass now, and go. I'm tired."

Jessie bent down again and lowered the little lady from her high pillows.

"Call Maggie now," said Aunt Jane.

The girls went out quietly and called Maggie. They finished washing the dishes. Then they waited in the front room for Maggie.

"You see how she is," said the tired woman. "First she wants me, and then she doesn't. I think she is finally settled for the night. You might as well go to bed, too."

"A fine idea," said Jessie. "Where do you sleep?"

"In this room off the kitchen," said Maggie. "If you want anything in the night, you can come down."

"Thanks, Maggie," said Jessie. "We won't feel so strange here, knowing that."

"Well, thank you both," she answered. "It's wonderful to have someone nice to talk to."

The girls went up to their big room. They climbed into bed and talked awhile.

"How beautiful the stars are!" Violet said. "They seem so near."

"I have never seen stars so bright before," said Jessie. "It's because there are no other lights at all."

Just as they were going to sleep, Jessie laughed and said, "Violet, where do you suppose that young man went? The one on the train."

"I can't think," answered Violet. "He just disappeared in the air!"

"A Mystery Man really," said Jessie.

And so they fell asleep.

CHAPTER 5

A Day at the Ranch

Sam, the neighbor, woke the girls the next morning, bringing the milk. The girls could hear Maggie in the kitchen, "Shh, Shh! Sam Weeks! You'll wake those girls."

"I want to wake them," said Sam. "I want to see them." He began to whistle.

The girls laughed while they washed their faces in the big wash bowl in their room. They dressed quickly. They wanted to see Sam, too.

"Well, well!" he said, as they came into the kitchen. "I hear you came to see your Aunt Jane. Are you planning to stay here all summer?"

"Sam!" cried Maggie. "How do they know?"

"We really don't know how long we'll stay," said Jessie. "We don't know how long Aunt Jane will want us."

"I'm worried about you," Sam said. "I'm afraid you won't get enough food. Maggie had to eat at our house when she got real hungry."

"Well," answered Jessie, dropping some eggs into hot water, "We can buy food. Grandfather gave me some money."

"I hope your aunt will let you eat it after you get it," said Sam. He turned to go.

He stopped at the door and turned to Maggie. "A stranger got off the train last night," he said.

"Yes, we know!" cried both girls.

"That's right, you would know," said Sam.

"We call him our Mystery Man," said Jessie.

"He's a mystery, all right," said Sam. "I noticed him because not very many people get off that fast train."

Sam watched the three people sit down at the

pretty table. He turned and walked quickly out the kitchen door.

Jessie smiled as she poured hot milk on a piece of toast.

"A little salt," she laughed, "and Aunt Jane's breakfast is ready."

She carried the plate into Aunt Jane's bedroom.

"More food, I suppose," said Aunt Jane.

"That's right," said Jessie. "It's milk toast. Delicious! Now, while you eat, I'll tell you our plan. Maggie is taking us to the store this morning to buy food. And while we are near the station, we'll send a telegram to Grandfather. We'll tell him we are having a fine time."

"A fine time? Pooh!" said Aunt Jane.

"But it's true, Aunt Jane," said Jessie quietly. "We love the ranch already. It's a beautiful place!"

"I'm the only person who has ever really liked this ranch," her aunt said. She began to eat her breakfast. Jessie watched her.

"She seems almost starved. If she is hungry, why doesn't she want to eat?" Jessie said to herself.

Jessie picked up the empty plate and left the room quietly.

When Jessie came into the kitchen, she saw Maggie at the back door with the horse and wagon. To her surprise, Violet was already on the seat.

"Don't we lock the door?" she asked.

"No, we never do. Nobody ever comes here," said Maggie. "Go on, old boy!"

As the horse walked slowly along, the girls made up a telegram to send to their grandfather. Tom Young, the station agent, sent the telegram.

CENTERVILLE

"A telegram every day. Quite an exciting town!" he said.

Just then they heard a train whistle. "The train goes the other way every morning," said Maggie. "Do you want to watch it come in?"

They saw the train come into the station. Nobody got on and nobody got off.

"That's the way it always is," said Maggie. "Soon the train won't stop at Centerville any more. It doesn't pay."

Maggie and the girls went to the store. They bought enough groceries to last a week and loaded them into the wagon. The old horse walked even slower than usual going home, because of the load.

When they came back to the ranch, they found Aunt Jane very cross.

"Humph!" she said to Maggie. "You go off riding all over the country and leave me here alone so that anything can happen!"

"But, Miss Jane," Maggie said, "what could possibly happen to you out here?"

"I was nearly fooled into selling this ranch! That's what could happen," the little old lady answered.

"Now, Miss Jane, this must be another one of your strange ideas," Maggie said.

"Strange, is it? Well, look at this." She pulled a paper from beneath her pillow. Maggie and the girls came closer to the bed to see what it said. It was an offer to buy the ranch for ten thousand dollars.

"Think of it!" Aunt Jane said. "Ten thousand dollars for my ranch! But I told those three men that my ranch isn't for sale at any price. I have other plans for it."

"Dear Aunt Jane," said Violet softly, "do you mean three men came into your room?"

"Yes," replied Aunt Jane. "But don't *you* worry, my dear. I could manage them."

Aunt Jane leaned her head back on her pillows again.

"Go away, now. All this excitement has made me tired."

Maggie and the girls went into the kitchen.

"I'd think she would be glad to get rid of the place at any price," said Maggie.

"I'm glad she didn't sell it, though," said Violet. "It's such a beautiful ranch. I wonder what plans she has for it."

CHAPTER 6

Golden Chimney

"We'll have a real dinner today," laughed Jessie. "Maybe Aunt Jane will eat some of this good food if I don't give her too much."

"I doubt it," said Maggie. "She hasn't eaten a real meal in two years."

Jessie was right. Maggie was amazed when she saw Aunt Jane's empty dishes.

"You girls certainly have a way with you," she said. "I have never seen her eat so much."

After the dishes were washed, Jessie softly opened her aunt's door.

Again, Aunt Jane looked as if she had been lying there waiting for something to happen.

"Well," she said, "what do you want now?"

Jessie spoke softly, "Violet and I wonder if we could explore this house."

"Go ahead," said her aunt. "There are no secrets here that I know of."

"No mysteries?" laughed Jessie.

"No," said Aunt Jane. "There are no mysteries, but it is a strange house. You'll find that it was built a little at a time. There are really four parts to the house."

As Jessie started to go out, her aunt called, "Be sure to look at the big chimney on the other side of the house. It is the prettiest thing here. It was made of stone from our own mountains."

"We will," said Jessie.

The two girls smiled at each other and went into the front room.

"Let's explore the whole house," said Jessie.

Violet laughed.

"I wonder why we love to fix up old houses?"

The girls stepped into the front hall. They went across it to the other side and found themselves in a front room like the one they had just left.

"This side of the house is exactly like the other one!" said Jessie. "See, here is the kitchen, the little bedroom, two front rooms and a side door."

"Here is the chimney and the fireplace," said Violet. "Isn't it beautiful?"

"The stone is smooth and shiny!" cried Jessie.

"See the tiny spots of yellow! Could they be gold?"

"They look brighter yellow than gold," said Violet. "The black spots are pretty, too."

Upstairs they found eight bedrooms.

"What fun it would be to put on new paper and paint!" cried Jessie.

Violet had opened the door of the little room right over Aunt Jane's.

"Oh, what a beautiful room!" she whispered. "Do come and look!"

It was the loveliest room in the house. The old wall paper was soft rose color. The window had fine white curtains. The small bed was high, like the big one in their bedroom. But this one had a top, covered with white curtains like those in the window.

"I wonder who fixed this room," said Violet. "Wouldn't it be pretty with violets on the wallpaper? I would love to live in this room."

"It looks just like you, Violet," said Jessie.

The girls finished their exploring and went back downstairs.

When they walked back to the kitchen, they heard Aunt Jane calling Maggie. Violet went in to see what she wanted.

"Did you see the chimney?" asked her aunt.

"Yes," said Violet. "It is beautiful."

"The stones came from our mountains," said Aunt Jane. "We thought once that those mountains were full of gold, but the gold was not real."

"The yellow and black spots make the chimney look very pretty, though," Violet said.

"Yes. That was one reason why my father used the stones for the chimney," her aunt answered. "And he also said that the chimney would always be a lesson to him. Every time he looked at it he could remember how he had to work hard for anything worth having. That way, he wasn't too disappointed that he had not found a lot of gold."

"This is really a beautiful house," Violet said. "There are so many pretty things here. Tell me, Aunt Jane, who fixed the little bedroom right over this one?"

Aunt Jane was very quiet for a minute. Violet thought she was not going to answer. Then she said,

"That was my room once," she said. She had tears in her eyes.

CHAPTER 7

The Boys Come

Two days passed before Maggie finally spoke her mind. She was feeling much better now with three delicious meals a day. And she enjoyed having someone to talk to.

Maggie and the two girls were sitting on the back steps, enjoying the cool evening breeze. The dinner dishes were done, and the first stars had come out over the ranch.

"Maybe I haven't any right to ask," Maggie began. "But I wonder what your grandfather is going to do about your aunt. She needs some care all the time. You girls can't stay here all summer."

"Maybe we can," said Violet softly. "We love it here, and I think Aunt Jane is used to having us now."

"There is one thing that's missing, though," said Jessie.

"Yes, I know," said Violet. "We both miss the boys."

Violet looked very sad.

"Maybe Aunt Jane would let the boys come, too," said Jessie. "Then it would be perfect." She looked at her sister.

"Let's ask her tomorrow," Violet said.

The two girls went upstairs to bed.

Next morning Jessie took a fine breakfast into her aunt's room. The little lady began to eat, and Jessie sat down beside the bed.

"We miss Henry and Benny, Aunt Jane," she began. "Couldn't we ask them to come for a few days? I'm sure Grandfather would let them come if you were willing."

"Well," said her aunt, "I'd agree to that."

The little lady looked up from her breakfast.

"But I don't want to see James, remember that!" she said.

"Grandfather is really very nice when you get to know him," said Jessie.

Aunt Jane gave a short laugh. "Don't forget that I knew your grandfather long before you did. If these two boys turn out like *him*, back they go!"

Jessie was sorry to hear her aunt talk like that. She did not answer. It was the best thing she could have done. Miss Jane was beginning to love the smiles on these two young faces.

What could she say to make Jessie happy again? she wondered.

"Tell Benny to bring his dog," she said.

What a smile came over Jessie's face! She did not say that Watch was not Benny's dog, but hers.

She said, "Oh, that's wonderful! Watch will love this ranch! And we'll keep him out of your room, I promise."

"Well, don't promise that," said Aunt Jane. "I like dogs in my room if they are good dogs."

"Watch is a wonderful dog," said Jessie. "He saved our lives once."

The girls went to the station and sent their daily telegram. The very next day they got an answer from Benny. His telegram said, "Henry and I will come on the same train you did. Bringing Watch. Bringing you more clothes. Love to Aunt Jane. Benny."

What a happy family it was when the four children were finally together in Aunt Jane's kitchen!

"You take the boys right in to see Aunt Jane,"

said Jessie, holding Watch by a strap. "I'll keep Watch with me."

The boys followed Violet into the bedroom. Aunt Jane was almost sitting up against her pillows. Her blue eyes were very bright.

"Hello, Aunt Jane," said Benny, going over to the bed. "I'm Benny. And aren't you a cute little lady!"

Aunt Jane was taken by surprise. She almost smiled.

"And I suppose you are Henry," she said.

"Yes. We are sorry you are sick," Henry answered. He hardly knew what to say to this strange woman.

"Who said I was sick?" asked Aunt Jane. "Well, you certainly don't look like your grandfather."

"No, I'm afraid not," said Henry.

"No need to be afraid about that," answered Aunt Jane. "I'm glad you don't look like him. And where's that big dog I've heard about?"

"Jessie, bring in Watch," called Henry.

Everyone watched to see what the dog would do.

He walked over to the bed and looked at the little old woman. Then he sat down and put out his paw.

"He wants to shake hands!" cried Benny, delighted. "Shake hands with him, Aunt Jane! You don't want to hurt his feelings."

For a minute, the children thought their aunt was angry. But to their surprise, she sat up and shook hands with the dog.

"Good dog," she said, lying back again.

Watch threw back his head and looked at Jessie. His mouth was open.

"Oh, Aunt Jane, he's laughing!" cried Benny. "He likes you!"

"Well, well," said Aunt Jane. "I'm glad the dog likes me, at least. You can go now and eat. And shut the door when you leave. I'm very tired from all the excitement."

The children went back into the kitchen and sat around the table, talking.

"Isn't Aunt Jane a surprise?" asked Jessie.

"She certainly is," said Henry, "but I like her."

Jessie said, "Just guess what I think. Which one of us will do the most to make Aunt Jane well again?"

And three voices answered together, "Watch!"

CHAPTER 8

Aunt Jane's Nurse

The next day was one of Aunt Jane's bad days. The boys went off gladly to look at the ranch, when they saw how cross she was.

"Now, Jane," the girls heard Maggie say, "You let me wash your hands and face."

"No!" was the sharp answer. Watch looked at the door and raised one ear.

"I don't know what to do with you," cried Maggie. "No breakfast. No washing. No clean bed. What do you want me to do?

"Do you want the window open?"

"No. This room is too cold already," the little lady said.

"You said a minute ago that it was too hot."

"Well, it was, a minute ago."

"Oh, dear me," said Maggie.

The girls looked at each other. The dog stood up and looked at the door. Violet put the last pile of dishes in the cupboard. Suddenly Maggie came from the bedroom. She shut the door behind her. She was almost crying.

"Girls, I can't do a thing with your aunt today. She was like this all the time before you came, but I did think she was getting over it."

"I wonder what she would say to me if I went in," said Violet. "I'd like to try."

"Are you sure?" asked Jessie. "Maybe she would be cross to anyone today."

"Never mind if she is, Jessie," answered her sister. "It won't hurt me."

"Of course it will hurt you, if she says mean things!" cried Jessie. "And it will hurt me, too."

"I'd still like to try," said Violet. "Just let me have the soap."

Violet knocked softly on the door to her aunt's bedroom.

"It's Violet, Aunt Jane. May I come in?"

"All right. Come in," said her aunt.

Violet went in quietly and put some newspapers in the chair by her aunt's bed. On the papers she put the big washbowl. Into the bowl, Violet poured hot water.

"It's such a hot day," she began pleasantly. "I think hot water makes you feel cooler, don't you?"

"Well, maybe," said Aunt Jane. She watched the pretty little girl.

"I've been sick a lot myself," Violet went on. "And one of my nurses told me that."

Violet took one of the thin little hands and washed it gently with hot soapy water. Then she dried it on a soft towel.

"I take care of the family when they are sick," said Violet. "Someday I am going to be a nurse."

She washed the other hand. Then she pushed Aunt Jane's white hair back and washed her face.

She was drying her aunt's face when Watch walked slowly into the room, wagging his tail. Aunt Jane looked at him.

"I don't feel like playing with you today," she said. "Go right back to the kitchen!"

Without a sound, Watch started for the kitchen. Then he turned and looked at Violet.

Violet said, "You're a nice dog, Watch, and I love you. But Aunt Jane said for you to go back to the kitchen."

Watch gave them both a look and turned sadly to go. His tail did not wag.

"Never mind!" cried Aunt Jane. "Come back! You can stay! I never saw a dog that minds as well as you do. Come here if you want."

Watch almost jumped across the room. He put his paws up on the white bed.

"No!" said Violet.

"Yes!" said Aunt Jane.

"We *never* let Watch get up on the beds," said Violet softly.

"I *always* let my dog lie on my bed," said Aunt Jane.

Watch looked first at one and then at the other.

"Up!" said Aunt Jane.

Watch gave a great jump and landed on the other side of the little lady. He lay down and put his head on his paws. He was not sure that he had done the right thing. He kept looking at Violet.

Violet was watching her aunt smile at Watch. She was sure that Watch had done the right thing.

CHAPTER 9

The Yellow Stones

Now that the children were together, they were very happy. Aunt Jane seemed to be getting more cheerful every day.

One morning Jessie heard her aunt call her.

"I want to see all four of you children," Aunt Jane told Jessie. "Get the others in here before I am tired again."

In a few minutes, the children were sitting in their aunt's room. Watch lay down at Jessie's feet and put his head on his paws. Only his eyes moved. He was very still.

"Now I want you to listen carefully," said Aunt Jane, looking at each of them in turn. "What I have to say is very important."

Since the children couldn't be more quiet than they already were, they sat and waited for her to go on.

"I'm going to give you children this ranch. No, don't say a word! You are the only relatives I have. You seem to be good children, and you have been kind to me."

The children were too surprised to say anything.

"I know you are not old enough to manage the ranch alone," she said, "so I'm going to bring Sam Weeks into it. He will manage the ranch for you. Mr. Pond, who handles my business, says that will be all right. Now, what have you to say to that?"

Henry was the first to speak. "We're too surprised to say much, Aunt Jane! It's wonderful!"

Watch got up and went over to the bed. He sat down and held out his paw. Aunt Jane took his paw and said, "I see you think this is a good idea.

If Watch thinks that, I am sure it must be true."

She patted the dog and went on, "The ranch is yours from this minute. All I have to do is write my name when Mr. Pond brings the papers. I want my ranch to belong to people who love it. That's why I wouldn't sell it to those three men."

The four children said "thank you" very softly, as they left.

"The only thing about this that I don't like is Grandfather," Benny said. He threw himself down on the grass.

"You said that wrong, old fellow," said Henry. "But we know what you mean. It leaves Grandfather out."

"I believe some day Aunt Jane will like him," said Violet, "and he will like her."

"I hope so," said Jessie.

They sat on the grass and looked at their ranch. The driveway came to the back door. It went past the windmill, past the barn, and then out again to the road. They could see woods and mountains.

They could see the long chicken houses from where they were sitting.

"Who were the men Aunt Jane was talking about?" asked Henry.

"Three men came while we were buying groceries," Violet answered. "They tried to make Aunt Jane sell the ranch to them."

"She probably needed the money," said Henry. "But I'm glad she gave the ranch to us instead of selling it. I hope she won't be sorry."

Benny said thoughtfully, "I think we ought to explore right away. If this is our ranch, we should know everything that's on it."

Jessie said, "Well, we could explore today. Let's ask Aunt Jane where to go."

The cross little lady was very pleased when the children asked her about their walk. No one had asked her advice for years.

"The first thing is, don't get lost. Go down past the chicken houses and you will come to some woods. Go through the woods and you come to an

open field. There is a stream. Follow that stream and you'll come right back home."

Benny said, "I think we should take a lunch, don't you, Aunt Jane?"

"By all means," said Aunt Jane, trying to hide a smile.

It was very hot in the sun. The children went down past the chicken houses. They came to the cool, green woods.

"It's a beautiful place," said Henry.

"A very nice place to eat lunch, too," said Benny.

The others laughed. But they were always hungry. They found a place where they could sit down. It was quiet and cool. Jessie was eating the last of her sandwich when she stopped, suddenly.

"Look, Henry!" she whispered. She pointed to some bushes not far away. "There's a little hut."

Henry got to his feet quickly. "The door is open," he said. "It seems to be empty."

The children went slowly toward the hut. There was nothing in it. But in front of it, there was a fireplace made of stones, almost hidden by the bushes. Henry put his hand down and felt the stones. Watch sniffed and wagged his tail.

"Well, let's be going," said Henry. "It looks to me as if someone built a fire here, and not too long ago, either."

The children walked faster now. Soon they came out in a big field filled with rocks and stones.

"There's no grass here," said Benny. "This field isn't very good, I would say."

"But it's very pretty," said Violet. "See the yellow and black lines in those rocks."

"These stones are yellow, too," said Jessie. She picked up a handful of the stones. As she dropped one, it broke into a fine yellow powder.

"They seem to be made of yellow sand," said Henry. "How queer!"

CHAPTER 10

A Big Present

When Sam came with the milk next day, he was surprised to see all four children on the back steps. They were waiting for him.

"Well, well! Early birds!" he said. "Why did you get up so early?"

"We wanted to see you, Sam," said Henry.

"Here I am, but I'm not much to look at," laughed Sam.

"Yes you are, Sam," said Benny. "I think you are a very fine looking man. And besides, we want to talk to you."

"Wait until I feed the chickens, and I'll be glad to sit down and talk."

The children went with Sam to the chicken houses and watched him.

"We want to know just how you do things," said Jessie. "So please show us."

Sam was glad to show them how to feed the chickens, give them water, and get the eggs.

In a little while, they were all sitting on boxes in the big open door of the barn.

Henry spoke up, "Aunt Jane says she is going to give us this ranch."

"*Give* you her ranch?" cried Sam. He could not believe his ears. "You are too young to own a ranch."

"Mr. Pond says we aren't, if you would be our boss," said Benny.

"Mr. Pond?" asked Sam. "Did he come here?"

"No, but he wrote letters to Aunt Jane," said Henry. "He knows about things like that, Aunt Jane says."

"He would know. But I still can't believe it."

Sam shook his head. "Just the same," he went on, "I'd like to have a chance to fix up this old place! Now, if we had some money, I could start a good egg business for you."

Sam stopped and shook his head again. "But I still can't believe it," he said.

"You'll just have to believe it, Sam," said Henry. "Aunt Jane said the ranch is ours right now. All she has to do is sign some papers."

Sam picked a blade of grass and chewed on it. He was upset at this strange news.

"What would we do after we got the egg business started?" asked Jessie.

"Well, I'd raise wheat. There are about five hundred acres on this ranch that would grow wheat."

"How big is this ranch?" asked Henry.

"The fields go way over to the mountains. Your aunt owns all that land."

"We never thought anything like this would happen when we came to see Aunt Jane," said Jessie.

The children and Sam sat looking at the big ranch that would soon be theirs.

"There's another surprise!" Sam said. "I've seen your Mystery Man!"

"Oh, where is he?" asked Jessie.

"He is still in town, but no one knows why. We never have strangers in Centerville, and everyone wonders why he is there."

"Haven't you any police in Centerville?" asked Henry. "I think this man ought to be watched."

"Oh, no, Henry," said Jessie quickly. "If you ever saw him, you wouldn't think that!"

"Well, we never had a policeman here, anyway," said Sam. "No need of one. But there is a sheriff in Stony Creek. That's the next town. His name is Bates."

"Look what's coming!" cried Benny. "A car!"

"It's Mr. Pond, sure as I live!" said Sam. "I guess this story of yours must be true."

"Mr. Pond is certainly early," said Jessie, laughing. "We haven't had breakfast."

Watch got to his feet and stood still, looking at the stranger. Then he began to wag his tail a very little.

"Good morning, Sam!" called Mr. Pond. He came slowly toward the barn.

Watch did not bark. He walked slowly toward the strange man, wagging his tail more and more.

"Well, hello. What's your name?" Mr. Pond asked the dog. "Are you a good dog?"

Benny said, "His name is Watch, and he is a very good dog. But he almost always barks at strangers."

"Well, see that you don't bark at me, old boy,"

said Mr. Pond. He patted Watch. Then he looked at the children with a nice smile.

"Your aunt sent for me," he said. "Suppose we go in and get this business done. You come too, Sam. Miss Jane doesn't like to wait, when she has made up her mind."

Henry said, "Will you wait just a minute, Mr. Pond? We want to talk to you before we see Aunt Jane."

Mr. Pond said, "I suppose you are Henry."

"Yes, sir. I am. We'd love to have this ranch. But it's all Aunt Jane has, and we don't want to take it away from her. Do you understand?"

"That's very fine," said Mr. Pond, nodding. "I can fix that easily. I can add a line saying that the money you get from the ranch will be used to take care of your aunt as long as she lives. Is that what you mean?"

"We'll feel better that way," said Jessie. "Of course, we would *do* it anyway. But it's nice to have it in writing."

They walked to the house where Maggie met them at the door.

"I am glad to see you, Mr. Pond," she said. "Jane can't wait a minute when she wants anything. She keeps asking why you haven't come."

"It won't take very long," said Mr. Pond, with a nice smile for Maggie. "I have all the papers right here with me. I'll just put in another line that Henry wants."

As Mr. Pond promised, it did not take long. Aunt Jane wrote her name. The four children wrote their names. Sam wrote his. And Mr. Pond was last.

In ten minutes, the ranch was owned by the four Alden children. Sam Weeks was the manager.

"Isn't it funny," said Benny, "what you can do by just writing your name?"

Mr. Pond laughed. "It gave you children twelve hundred and eighty acres of land, and a big ranch house."

"And a hut, too," said Benny, "where someone has been staying."

"What? What's that?" asked Aunt Jane. "I didn't know there was a hut on my land."

"We didn't want to worry you," said Henry. "But we did find a hut in the woods. And it looks as if somebody built a fire there."

"We didn't see anyone, though," said Jessie.

Mr. Pond looked very serious. Then he smiled and said, "I'm sure it's nothing to worry about. Now, you eat your breakfast and let me talk to Sam."

The two men went out. They stood by the car for a long time talking, while Jessie got breakfast. She would have been surprised if she had known what they were saying. She would have been excited, too. For they were not talking about the ranch, but about the man on the train and the hut in the woods.

Jessie fixed a breakfast tray and took it into her aunt's room. This morning Jessie did not ask her aunt to eat. She just put the tray down in front of the little woman. Miss Alden ate bacon and toast and an egg without saying a cross word.

"Aunt Jane," said Jessie, "You'll never be sorry that you gave us your ranch. We love it. We will take care of it. We love you, too, and we will always take care of you, even after we go home."

Aunt Jane sighed. No one had ever *wanted* to take care of her before. She looked very happy.

"I feel safe, now," she said. "I know that my ranch will be taken care of by people who love it."

CHAPTER 11

A Strange Offer

That night Henry did not sleep very well. He kept thinking of the men who had tried to buy Aunt Jane's ranch. He decided to talk with Jessie alone.

But it was not easy for the older children to get away from Benny. He wanted to do first one thing and then another. Finally he wanted to go to the barn to see the horse.

"It's our horse, after all," said Benny. "We ought to get acquainted with our own horse."

Watch began to bark when Violet let him out the back door.

"Bark all you want to, Watchie!" shouted Benny. "Nobody can hear you, and I'll yell, too!"

After a few good yells, Benny started toward the barn. All the children followed. Watch ran around the old barn looking for mice. The black horse stood looking at them all.

"What's our horse's name?" asked Benny.

"Maggie says he hasn't any name," said Jessie. "She just says, 'Go on, old boy.' "

"Old Boy isn't a good name," said Benny. "Let's call him Snowball."

Everyone laughed. The thin old horse was black all over! But from then on, Old Boy was called Snowball.

"Come on, Watch," said Benny at last. "Let's go upstairs where the hay is. Maybe you'll find a rat!"

Violet followed Benny and this gave Henry his chance. He winked at Jessie who followed him outside at once.

"Look, Jessie," whispered Henry. "I don't like the idea of strange men bothering Aunt Jane."

"Neither do I," said Jessie softly. "The men told her the ranch was no good. Just a few chickens and an old horse."

"That's it," cried Henry. "If the ranch is no good, why do they want to buy it? I think I ought to do something about this."

"Tell Sam," advised Jessie.

"I'll do better than that," said Henry at last. "I'll tell Sam to tell Mr. Pond. Mr. Pond seems to know everything."

After they had told their troubles to Sam, the older children felt better. They were pleased when they saw Sam start for Mr. Pond's house.

In a very short time, Mr. Pond's car came up the driveway. Sam was with him. They were both very serious.

"Sam and I want to see that hut in the woods," Mr. Pond said. "Will you take us there?"

"Sure," said Henry. "We know exactly where it is."

"Let's all go," cried Benny.

Jessie went to the front hall and told Maggie where they were going.

"Don't tell Aunt Jane that we are going back to that hut. It would worry her. Just say we went for a walk. We will be back in time for dinner."

Jessie saw the others half way to the chicken house. She hurried to catch up with them. They walked faster this time, because they knew just where they were going. They soon came to the hut.

"Be quiet, now," whispered Sam, "We want to see if anyone is here."

The children sat down in the woods.

"Is there anything different about the hut?" whispered Mr. Pond.

"Yes," whispered Henry. "There is some wood in the fireplace. It wasn't there the other time."

They sat very still for a long time. They heard nothing. They saw nothing new.

"Well," said Mr. Pond at last, "we might sit here all day for nothing. Let's take a close look at the hut."

They walked over to the hut. Sam put his hand on the stones of the fireplace.

"Warm!" he said.

They all felt the stones. They were very warm. The fire had not been out very long.

"Well, someone surely stays here," said Mr. Pond. He seemed worried.

"Do you suppose it's your Mystery Man?" asked Benny.

"Goodness no!" Jessie answered. "He's much too nice to live in a hut on somebody else's land."

They walked out of the woods and into the field full of rocks.

"Aren't these rocks funny?" said Violet. "I never saw such yellow rocks. And look at the black lines across them!"

"Like a tiger," said Benny.

Henry looked again at the rocks. He seemed to be deep in thought.

"Now what is it they make me think of?" he said to himself. "Umm, yellow with black lines. . . . I

have seen something about that somewhere. . . ."

"Do you know the name of these yellow stones, Mr. Pond?" asked Violet. She picked one up and gave it to him.

"No, I don't know much about stones," he said. "This yellowish rock makes a fine powder. I know that Indians long ago used it for their sand paintings."

"Sand paintings?" asked Benny. "I never heard of sand paintings."

"They are very interesting," said Mr. Pond. "They are beautiful, too. The Indians took sand of all colors: blue, green, red, yellow, black, brown. They looked for a nice, flat place, and painted it with colored sand. They put the different colors in the right places. They would make a round sun like this."

Mr. Pond quickly made a big yellow sun on the ground, to show Benny how it was done.

"Do you think there are any sand paintings in our field now?" Benny asked hopefully.

"No," answered Mr. Pond, smiling. "There haven't been any Indians here for many years."

"I'd rather have Indians here than whoever is living in that hut," said Jessie.

"I think you're right," said Mr. Pond. "But don't worry about that. We'll go to Stony Creek tomorrow and tell the sheriff, Mr. Bates, about this."

He glanced at Henry, and the boy understood that Mr. Pond would tell the sheriff about some other things, too.

CHAPTER 12

The Mystery Man

Early the next morning, the four Alden children climbed into Mr. Pond's car. He had come to take them to Stony Creek. They were going to see the sheriff, Mr. Bates.

Mr. Pond was very quiet. He was worried about these nice children. He liked them, even though he had only known them a short time. And he was worried about Jane Alden, too. He had known her for many years. He knew well enough that she had always been cross and hard to get along with. But he was very sorry for her. He didn't want any of them to be upset by these three strange men.

They drove up in front of the courthouse in Stony Creek and Mr. Pond stopped the car.

"Come right in," called Mr. Bates. "I'm glad you came. I don't often have so much company."

"Hello, Bates," said Mr. Pond. "These are the Alden children."

"I had already guessed that," said Mr. Bates. He took his guests to a small back room and shut the door.

They all sat down.

"Well, what brings you here?" asked Mr. Bates.

Mr. Pond said, "We came to see you about police business. There is something going on in the Alden woods. It looks as if someone has been living in an old hut there."

Mr. Bates didn't look surprised. He just waited for Mr. Pond to go on.

"That isn't all," Mr. Pond said. "Three strange men tried to make Miss Jane Alden sell her ranch. They told her it was no good. Say, Bates, you act as if you knew something that I don't. What do you really think about all this?" Mr. Bates just sat and smiled.

"Maybe you won't have to worry about those men any longer," he said. "And I don't think anyone will be staying in that hut, either. But I'll wait and let Mr. Carter tell you all about it."

"Mr. Carter? Who would that be?" asked Benny.

"He is a very important man," Mr. Bates said, still smiling. "Here he comes now."

A car stopped just behind Mr. Pond's. A good-looking young man got out. He was very tall. He had soft brown hair. When he stood in the door, Jessie and Violet looked at him with their mouths open. Then they looked at one another.

Jessie could hardly talk. "Oh, Violet," she whispered, "Our Mystery Man!"

"Are you surprised?" asked Mr. Carter, laughing.

"We certainly are," said Benny. "We thought you might be a bad man. That is, Henry thought so, anyway."

"Benny!" Henry said, blushing. "I didn't really think that, Mr. Carter. I just thought the police should—I mean—well, you were a stranger, and—"

"That's all right, Henry," said the Mystery Man, smiling again. "That was a smart thing to think."

"But if you're not a bad man, who are you?" asked Benny.

"Well, I've been working for you, but you didn't know it."

"Working for us?" asked Benny. "You don't look like a ranch hand."

"There are many ways to work," Mr. Carter said. "And one of them is looking for uranium."

"Uranium!" Jessie cried. She had finally found her voice again.

"Yes," said Mr. Carter. "My job is to look for uranium. I found a field of it right on your ranch."

"Do you mean that all of that Indian dust is really uranium?" asked Violet.

"It certainly is," Mr. Carter answered, looking at all the surprised faces around him.

"But why were you looking there?" asked Violet. "And who are those three tough men?"

Mr. Carter answered slowly, "I work for a man you may have heard of. Mr. Alden of Greenfield."

"Grandfather!" the children cried.

"Yes. Mr. Alden hired me to look for uranium for him. There is a lot of it in this part of the country. But when I found it on your ranch, I also found that someone had been there first."

"That must be those three men!" Henry said.

"Yes. They were looking for uranium, too. But they are not honest. When they found a place that had uranium, they tried to buy the land cheap. They didn't tell people what they had found."

"That's just what they tried to do to us," Violet said.

"Yes," Mr. Carter went on, "but Mr. Bates and I caught up with them. You won't be bothered by them again."

"Are they the ones who stayed in that hut on our ranch?" asked Jessie.

"Yes. But I had an eye on them. They couldn't have hurt you," Mr. Carter said.

Henry spoke slowly, "This means that the ranch is worth a lot of money, doesn't it?"

"It certainly does," said Mr. Carter.

"Wait till I tell Aunt Jane!" shouted Benny.

"Can we tell people?" asked Henry.

"I suppose so," said Mr. Carter. "It is no longer a secret. I'm afraid your ranch will not be quiet much longer. Your place will soon be full of strangers. Maybe some of them will try to take rocks away from your uranium fields." He looked worried for the first time since he had come in the door.

"What can we do?" asked Jessie. "It would be terrible to upset Aunt Jane just when she is getting better."

"Can you help them, Mr. Pond?" asked Mr. Carter.

"No, I'm afraid not," said Mr. Pond. "It is too big a job for me. I think the children need a smarter man than I am. And they need someone with enough money to dig a mine."

Henry said, "I think I know the very man."

The four children shouted together, "Grandfather!"

CHAPTER 13

Fast Work

Mr. Carter spoke, "I think your grandfather will be glad to help. I can go to Greenfield and tell him the whole story."

He looked at his watch and got up quickly. "Good-by, children, and the best of luck."

In one minute he was gone.

Benny said, "Mystery men work fast, don't they?"

"There's just one thing wrong," Henry said. "Aunt Jane didn't want Grandfather to come to her ranch. Maybe she will be angry if he comes to help us."

"Well, maybe she will be good and glad!" said Mr. Pond, laughing. "She ought to be thankful if he will come. She won't like it when people begin to go across her land."

The children were quiet all the way home. They were wondering how to tell Aunt Jane.

"Let's not worry," said Violet at last. "Things always work out all right for us."

But even Violet was in for a surprise.

Watch met them at the door, barking and wagging his tail. Maggie was smiling in the kitchen. Aunt Jane was laughing at them from the front room! She was sitting in her long chair, all dressed. The children had never seen her in a dress before.

"Dear Aunt Jane!" cried Violet. "You are up and dressed! I was never so glad in my life." She bent over and kissed the little old lady.

Aunt Jane was surprised at the kiss. But she was very pleased.

"I will bring the kitchen table in here," said Henry.

"Why not eat on the table that is in here?"

"But that is your very best table," said Jessie.

"It is your table, remember," said Aunt Jane. "I'd like to eat on it, if you want to use it."

A happy family sat down to supper that night.

"Now, tell me everything that happened in Stony Creek," said Aunt Jane.

The children took turns. They told her everything. They told her what a fine man the Mystery Man was. They passed quickly over the three tough men, because they did not want to frighten her.

"They caught them anyway," said Benny, "So no more trouble from them."

At last, everything had been told except one thing —Grandfather.

"About these strangers," said Benny. "Mr. Carter says this place won't be quiet any more. Everyone will come to see the uranium. And maybe some will take away rocks."

Aunt Jane nodded. "What does he think we ought to do?"

"He says we can't take care of it ourselves," began Henry. "We must have help from some man who can do things in a big way and who has money to have a mine dug."

Aunt Jane said slowly, "I know one man who can do it. My brother, James."

For a minute the children could not speak. Then Jessie cried, "Oh, he could, Aunt Jane!"

"And now I wonder if he *would*," said Aunt Jane, "after the way I've treated him."

"I'm sure he would," said Jessie excitedly.

"Well, I hope so," said her aunt. "I could never stand hundreds of people running all over my ranch—your ranch. I'll send your grandfather a night letter."

"If you will write a night letter," said Henry, "I'll take it to Tom Young's house and have him send it tonight."

"You care a lot for your grandfather, don't you?" asked the old lady, with a sharp look.

"And we care a lot for you, too," said Henry.

"Get me some paper at once, Henry," said Aunt Jane, "before I change my mind."

The children were very quiet while their aunt wrote the night letter. They were afraid every minute that she would change her mind.

"Listen to this," she said at last. " 'Will you take over all business of the uranium fields, now owned by your grandchildren? For once I am glad to have you for a boss. The children and Watch send love. Jane.' "

"Perfect!" said Henry.

Next morning, right after breakfast, a telegram came for Aunt Jane.

She read it aloud, " 'I shall be glad to take over this business. You do not have to see me. Decide how much land you want to keep for yourself and we will build a fence around it. I will send a guard for the house. James Alden.' "

"A guard for this house!" cried Benny. "Isn't this exciting!"

Jessie called, "Look! Here's a car already!"

The car was full of telephone men. One of them asked Aunt Jane very politely where she wanted the telephones.

"Telephones?" asked Benny. "Are you going to put in two?"

"We have to put in four," he said. "I guess you folks don't know what you are in for."

"No, I guess we don't," said Henry. "I think I had better go to town and telephone Grandfather now. I may not have a chance later."

Henry left with Watch.

How wonderful it was to talk with Grandfather!

"Now, listen carefully," Mr. Alden said, "Your aunt's ranch must always be kept a pleasant place for her to live. So, when you have time, let her decide where the fence should go. Then she could always do anything she wanted with the ranch itself. Do you understand?"

"I think so. You mean we still might want to run the ranch?"

"Exactly."

Henry noticed that his grandfather still called the ranch "hers." He also knew that he must get right at the fence. When his grandfather said, "When you have time," he meant right away.

Henry went back to the ranch and told his aunt what Mr. Alden had said.

"Grandfather wants us to decide where that fence shall go."

"I know already," said the little lady. "Here is a plan of the ranch. I have marked where I want the fence to go."

Aunt Jane listened. "Here comes another car," she said.

"Poor Aunt Jane!" said Jessie. "You'll never get any rest."

"That's Grandfather for you," said Benny.

The men were sent by Mr. Alden to put up the fence. Henry was glad that his aunt had the plan ready in time.

Jessie asked, "Do you want Henry to carry you to bed, Aunt Jane?"

"No. I want him to help me to the kitchen window, so I can see the cars drive up. I want to see everything."

Henry took her to a big easy chair by the kitchen window.

"Doesn't Grandfather work fast?" asked Jessie.

"He always did," said her aunt. "Once he worked too fast for me. But not now. Here comes another car!"

"I just can't believe it," said Violet, "We'll never get any work done."

Benny came in to tell the news. His face was red with excitement.

"The guards are here!" he shouted. "They will stop people from knocking on our door all the time and asking us about the uranium. They say we will get tired of it. But I wouldn't, would you, Aunt Jane?"

"I'm not tired of it yet," said Aunt Jane.

CHAPTER 14

The Boss

Boy, look at that car!" said Benny, looking out the window. It was long and low. It was painted yellow and black. A man got out of the car. A guard spoke to him and nodded, and the man came to the back door.

Henry opened the door, and the man said, "James Alden asked me to come and see his sister."

"Come in," said Henry. "This is my aunt."

The man smiled at the little old lady. "James Alden is one of my best friends," he said.

"Sit down," said Aunt Jane, in a kind voice. "We seem to have all our callers in the kitchen. Some day we may use the front door."

"The kitchen is all right with me," said the stranger, with a quick smile. "My name is Gardner. I am a mining man. Your brother sent me to take care of your uranium field."

Benny asked, "Are you the boss of everything?"

"That's a good way to put it," agreed Mr. Gardner.

"Will you let us watch you dig?" asked Benny.

"Yes. There are some men digging in your field now. Do you want to see them?"

"We certainly do!" said Henry at once.

They started across the field.

"Keep your eyes on that white place on the mountain. The hole is there," Mr. Gardner said.

When they came to the hole, they saw two guards beside it. Two other men were standing in the hole with long sticks in their hands.

"Those are geiger counters!" shouted Benny.

"That's right," said Mr. Gardner.

The men heard his voice and looked up. When they saw who it was, one of them came out of the hole.

"It's good, sir," he said. "Want to hear it?"

The boss listened. "Good!" he said. "Noisy, isn't it? Let the children listen. After all, they own the whole works."

Benny was so excited that he almost fell into the hole.

"How it snaps!" he said.

"There must be a lot of uranium here," said Henry, as he listened to the geiger counter pop.

When the children walked into the house again, Aunt Jane was sitting by the window in the front room.

"Did you have a good time?" she asked.

"Wonderful!" said Benny. "We listened to the geiger counter, and it made a terrible noise. That means uranium, Aunt Jane."

"Does it? I am glad to hear it." She seemed to be very pleased.

After dinner that evening the children left Violet alone with their aunt. Violet was sewing.

"Aunt Jane," she said gently, "I really don't understand why you didn't let your own brother help you when you needed money."

"I might as well tell you the whole story," said Aunt Jane. "Father and mother went East. Your grandfather was a very young man. He wanted to sell the ranch and go into the mill business."

"I begin to understand," said Violet softly.

"I'm glad somebody understands," said Aunt Jane. "I loved the ranch. So I said I'd stay here. But I couldn't run the ranch. I didn't know how. I had twenty men working for me. Then I had to let the men go, one by one. At last, only Sam was left. I sold the horses and cattle."

Aunt Jane paused. "How could I ask your grandfather for money? He never wanted me to stay here and I wouldn't give in and say that I was wrong."

"I'm glad you told me this, Aunt Jane. I'll help you get to bed, now."

Things happened fast on the Alden ranch in the next few weeks. A mine was dug. Big machines worked night and day. Houses for workmen were built. New stores opened in town. The train was not taken off. Instead, there were four trains every day. Two telephone girls stayed upstairs all day to answer the telephones. And Aunt Jane made a surprising announcement.

"I want to give a party!" she said.

"A party?" asked Henry. "When?"

"My birthday is next week, and I want a birthday party."

"People don't give their own birthday parties," said Henry. "Let us give the party for you."

"No," said Aunt Jane. "This is my party. And I am going to ask your grandfather if he will come!"

Violet said, "Oh, I'm so glad, Aunt Jane! I'm sure he will."

The children's wish had come true.

"Telephone to him!" shouted Benny.

Aunt Jane, her face very pink, called her brother.

"Hello, James," she said brightly. "I want you to come to my birthday party."

"Ahem!" said Grandfather. The children could hear his deep voice.

"Of course I will, if you want me. I'll bring you a present, too."

"No, just come, and forgive me for everything."

The children knew that Grandfather did not know what to say to this.

"Well, well!" he said, "Nothing to forgive!"

"Thank you, James," said Aunt Jane.

Mr. Gardner took the children to meet their grandfather's train, the day before Aunt Jane's birthday.

When the children saw Mr. Alden, what a noise they made! They all shouted at once. They rushed up and took his bags. Tom Young stood in the door of the station and laughed.

"They think a lot of *him*," he said.

They all piled into Mr. Gardner's car and drove to the ranch.

Aunt Jane was sitting up very straight in the front room. She shook hands with her brother.

"It was good of you to come, James," she said.

"I'm glad to see you," said Grandfather. "I had forgotten you were so pretty."

It was true. When the children looked at their aunt, they saw that she was really pretty. Her blue eyes were very bright.

Mr. Alden said, "I want to see Henry alone."

Henry and his grandfather went to the back room to talk. Grandfather came back alone. The children heard Henry drive out of the yard in Mr. Gardner's car. They were very surprised.

"Where is Henry going?" asked Aunt Jane.

"A secret," said Mr. Alden, laughing.

Henry came back in a little while. He nodded at his grandfather and said, "All right."

"What can it be?" wondered Jessie. "How can we wait until tomorrow?"

After supper, Grandfather said, "Jane, I have a plan. Do you want to hear it?"

"I do," said Aunt Jane. "It seems funny, doesn't it? I never would listen to you before."

"I was too bossy," said Mr. Alden. "I know that now." He smiled.

"My grandchildren love your ranch, Jane," he said, "but they can't stay here all winter."

"Yes, I know that, James," she said sadly.

"They want to fix up the other end of this house for Sam and his wife. We can cut a door between your room and the next one. Maggie can have that room. Then you will be safe all winter."

"You are kind to plan this for me," said Aunt Jane. She smiled kindly at her brother.

"The children planned it," said Mr. Alden. "They want to fix the rooms upstairs for themselves."

"Well, they certainly can," said Aunt Jane.

"Now, one last idea," said Mr. Alden. He looked at Jessie, with a twinkle in his eye.

"I heard all about your Mystery Man," he said.

"He's not *my* Mystery Man," said Jessie, laughing. "But he was nice, wasn't he?"

"He doesn't seem like a Mystery Man any more," said Violet. "I'd like to see him again sometime."

Mr. Alden said, "He *could* come to the party tomorrow, if anyone asked him."

"Very well," said Aunt Jane. "I don't mind having a Mystery Man at my birthday party."

"Will he fly?" asked Jessie.

"No. He is already here," said Grandfather. "He got off the train when I did!"

"And we didn't even see him," said Benny.

"Well, he is still a Mystery Man in some ways, isn't he?" said Violet.

CHAPTER 15

The Party

"It's the Mystery Man!" shouted Benny, looking out the window the next day. "I hope the guard will let him in."

It was John Carter, the tall young man with the brown hair and brown eyes. He went first to Aunt Jane and thanked her for asking him to come. Then he spoke to all the children as if he were delighted to see them.

"I want to show you something, Carter," said Mr. Alden. "You children come, too. We're going to look at the fireplace in the other kitchen."

"I won't go," said Aunt Jane, smiling. "I know all about that chimney."

When they stood before the fireplace, Mr. Alden said, "See that yellow and black in the stone, Carter?"

"Why, this is funny!" Mr. Carter said, "That fireplace is made of uranium ore! There is gold and silver in it, too."

"The gold and silver are not good," said Mr. Alden. "Of course, we had never heard of uranium when we built the chimney. I think that is the only chimney in the world that is made of uranium ore."

"Is the chimney the same all the way up?" asked Benny.

Grandfather laughed. "Yes, all the way up. We left it rough outside, and smoothed it inside. My father and mother and I went East, and we had a chimney right here with uranium in it!"

They went back to the living room.

Jessie said, "Aunt Jane, you remember you said there were no mysteries in this house? And in a way, that chimney was a fine mystery."

"I didn't know it then," said her aunt.

"We didn't know about the fields either," said Benny, "or who the Mystery Man was. Let's call this Mystery Ranch!"

"That's a fine name!" said Mr. Carter. "You could paint the name on a sign and hang it over the driveway."

At six o'clock, the birthday party began. Everyone was excited. Watch barked and barked, and nobody stopped him.

They set the big table with a white linen cloth. They set eight places with Aunt Jane's best dishes. The birthday cake had seventy tiny candles on it.

When supper was over, Aunt Jane said, "Take the dishes into the kitchen and leave them there. You can wash them later. I want to open my presents!"

The children had made their presents for Aunt Jane with loving hands. They sat, watching the pretty little lady.

Jessie thought, "How very different she is from the little old lady in bed! I'm glad we came here."

"I love every one of my presents!" cried Aunt Jane.

"Now let me get yours, Grandfather!" cried Henry.

"Very well, my boy," said Mr. Alden, smiling.

Henry rushed out to the barn. Soon he came back with a tiny black and white puppy in his arms. He put it on the floor. It was very soft. Watch stood up quickly and looked at it.

"Come here, Watch," said Jessie. "Be a good dog."

"Her name is Lady, Aunt Jane," said Henry.

"Oh, what a beautiful little dog!" said Aunt Jane. "Is she for me?"

"Yes," said Mr. Alden. "To take the place of Watch when the children go home."

Watch wagged his tail a little. He sat down.

"She's just a baby dog, Watch," said Jessie. "You be good, now."

"Do you want to hold the puppy, Aunt Jane?" asked Henry.

He put the little dog in her arms. Watch didn't like this. He sat and looked at the stranger.

Happy
Birthday

Aunt Jane loved it. Anyone could see that. The puppy loved her, too. It lay down against her arm and shut its eyes.

"Lady is tired," said Henry. "She goes to sleep whenever she can."

Aunt Jane sat very still. She held the baby dog quietly. She was very pleased when it went to sleep.

Watch lay down again, beside Jessie, as if to say, "Well, I don't care. After all, I'm Jessie's dog."

Grandfather looked at his family and his friends. He loved every one of his grandchildren. He was very happy now that he had a sister again.

Grandfather said to Mr. Carter, "This is a very happy day for me. You can see what fine grandchildren I have."

"You certainly do, Mr. Alden."

"Now we will all be happy next year," he went on. "The children will go back to school. Sam and Annie can move into this house. Maggie can stay happily with Jane. And best of all, I have a sister again."

But Aunt Jane shook her head and said, with tears in her eyes, "No, James. Best of all, I have a brother."

The Alden children just looked at one another. They were too happy to say a word.

GERTRUDE CHANDLER WARNER discovered when she was teaching that many readers who like an exciting story could find no books that were both easy and fun to read. She decided to try to meet this need, and her first book, *The Boxcar Children*, quickly proved she had succeeded.

Miss Warner drew on her own experiences to write the mystery. As a child she spent hours watching trains go by on the tracks opposite her family home. She often dreamed about what it would be like to set up housekeeping in a caboose or freight car—the situation the Alden children find themselves in.

When Miss Warner received requests for more adventures involving Henry, Jessie, Violet, and Benny Alden, she began additional stories. In each, she chose a special setting and introduced unusual or eccentric characters who liked the unpredictable.

While the mystery element is central to each of Miss Warner's books, she never thought of them as strictly juvenile mysteries. She liked to stress the Aldens' independence and resourcefulness and their solid New England devotion to using up and making do. The Aldens go about most of their adventures with as little adult supervision as possible—something else that delights young readers.

Miss Warner lived in Putnam, Connecticut, until her death in 1979. During her lifetime, she received hundreds of letters from girls and boys telling her how much they liked her books. And so she continued the Aldens' adventures, writing a total of nineteen books in the Boxcar Children series.